# The BIGGEST TEST
## in the Universe

Nancy Poydar

Holiday House / New York

www.holidayhouse.com
First Edition
1 3 5 7 9 10 8 6 4 2
ISBN-13: 978-0-8234-1944-9
ISBN-10: 0-8234-1944-4

**Library of Congress Cataloging-in-Publication Data**
Poydar, Nancy.
The biggest test in the universe / Nancy Poydar. – 1st ed.
p. cm.
Summary: Sam and his classmates dread Friday, the day they
are to take the infamous Big Test.
ISBN 0-8234-1944-4 (hardcover)
[1. Examinations – Fiction.  2. Schools – Fiction.]  I. Title.
PZ7.P8846Bi 2004
[E] – dc22                              2004060555

Designed by Yvette Lenhart

For Mary Cash

Sam was the luckiest boy in the universe. He had Mr. Albright for a teacher. Every year, Mr. Albright's class turned the whole room into the solar system! The only bad thing about this year was the Big Test. The Big Test tested everything you ever learned.

So on Monday, when Mr. Albright said, "Boys and girls, the Big Test is Friday," Sam stopped feeling lucky.

Everyone spoke at once. "The test with the answer sheet?" asked Alice.

"The test you have to pass to stay in school?" asked George.

"It has answer sheets. Everyone stays in school," said Mr. Albright.

"The Big Test is so hard, my brother says your head looks like a marble when it's over," cried Ed.

"I heard you get blisters on your brain!" claimed Kira.

"You've been practicing," said Mr. Albright. "No one should worry."

Sam worried anyway.

On Tuesday the older kids were talking on the playground.

"The Big Test booklet is like a **telephone book**," said Ben.

"**Nobody** finishes," said Isabel.

"When it's over, they put your arm in a **sling**!" said Ben.

"Some arms fall off!" shrieked Isabel.
"Do not!" said Sam, but he worried more.

On Wednesday Cousin Charlie said, "The Big Test was easy! I took it upside down just for fun."
　　"Did not," said Sam.

His grandfather said, "When I was a boy, they measured your head; and if it wasn't bigger at the end of the year, no graduating!"
　　"Not true!" said Sam.

His mother said, "When I was a girl, they made us write huge reports. It took weeks, and you slept at the school!"

"**DID NOT!**" shouted Sam.

Sam's father said, "Why are you so worried?"
"Just am," moaned Sam.

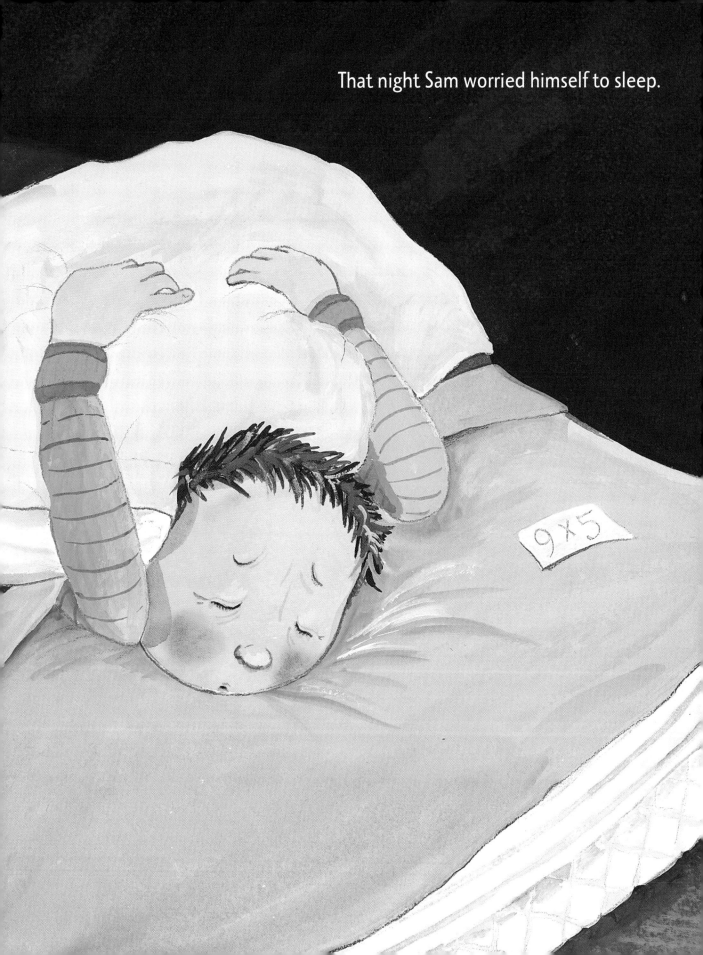

That night Sam worried himself to sleep.

On Thursday, the teachers made the older kids put up helpful hints. Sam wanted to cry. Tomorrow was the Big Test.

Friday morning, Sam said, "I'm sick today."

"Oh, dear," said his mother. "I'll have to sign you up for Big Test Makeup Day next Saturday. No pancakes today. No soccer next Saturday."

"I feel better," said Sam. He put on his lucky hat.

At school the desks were in rows instead of clustered in constellations. There were new pencils. Mr. Albright passed out the test booklets. Sam wished they were painting their planets. Mr. Albright said, "BEGIN."

Blast off! thought Sam.

A siren screamed in the street.

Mr. Albright shut the window.

I'm in outer space, Sam thought.

He knew answers.

He made a mistake!

Rub, rub went Sam's eraser. It made a black hole in his paper.

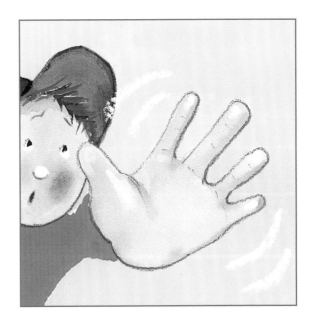

EMERGENCY!
   "Just go on," whispered Mr. Albright.

Alice blew her nose.

George snickered.

Mr. Albright glared.

Sam broke his pencil.
EMERGENCY!

Like a rocket, Mr. Albright
zoomed over with a new one.

Sam turned the page.

The end was at the bottom.

Finally Mr. Albright said, "PENCILS
DOWN."

Sam's pencil crashed onto his desk like a meteor.
Alice pretended her hand hurt. So did George.
Mr. Albright said, "It wasn't *that* bad."
"***Was too!***" they wailed.

"It wasn't *that* bad," said George to Sam after school.
"Nah!" said Sam. "It was **easy**. I took it **upside down** just for fun!"

George's little sister Elly caught up with them.
"How was the Big Test?"

"**Terrible!**" claimed Sam. "My arm is falling off!"

"The test booklet is like a **telephone book**!" said George.

"**Nobody** finished!" said Sam.

"It was so hard, your head turns into a **marble**!" said George.

"I'm going to be sick on Big Test day!" declared Elly.

"If you're sick they bring it to your house," warned Sam.

"Yeah," said George. "I know a kid who had to *eat* it!"

"Yuck!" cried Elly. "Sophie!" She gulped. "Some kids had to *eat* the Big Test!"

Sam was the luckiest boy in the universe. Now, he had two reasons. One, he had Mr. Albright for a teacher; and two, he had taken the Biggest Test in the Universe and **LIVED**!